A Sweet Meeting on Mimouna Night

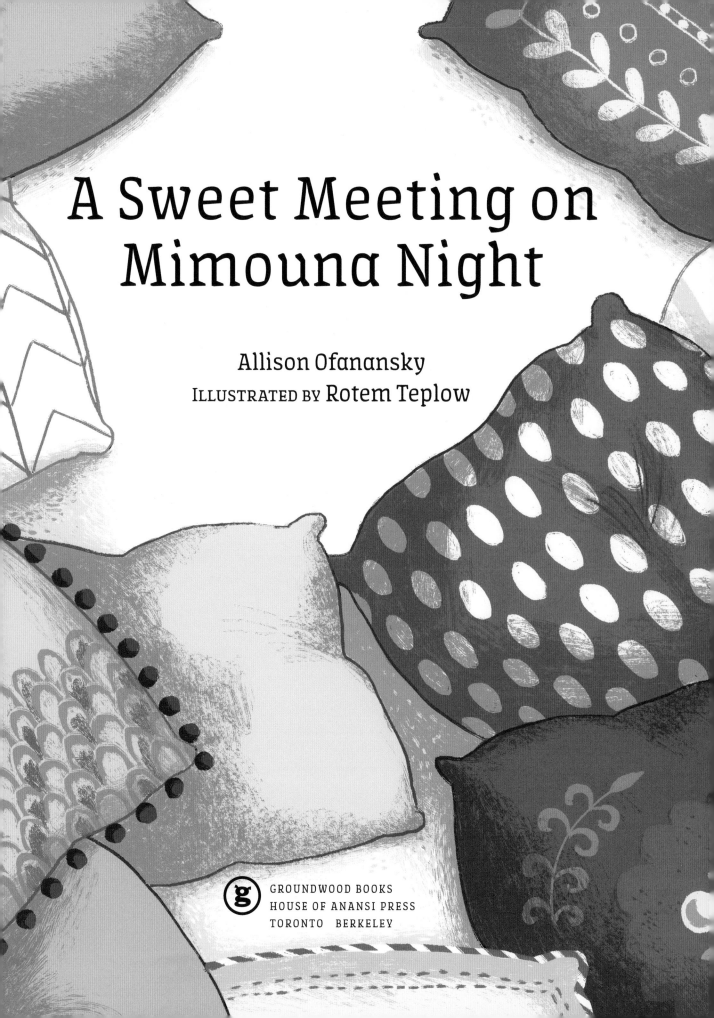

A Sweet Meeting on Mimouna Night

Allison Ofanansky

ILLUSTRATED BY Rotem Teplow

GROUNDWOOD BOOKS
HOUSE OF ANANSI PRESS
TORONTO   BERKELEY

It is the last afternoon of Passover. Miriam sits in her courtyard and watches the sky above the rooftops of Fes turn dark. When three stars twinkle overhead, Passover ends and another holiday — Mimouna — begins.

"I want to help make the moufletot!" she calls to her mother. After eating matzah all week, Miriam can't wait to sink her teeth into the paper-thin pancakes her mother always makes for Mimouna.

But before Passover, her family cleaned every crumb of bread and speck of flour out of the house. They can't have a Mimouna party without doughy treats!

"Where can we get flour tonight?"

In answer, Miriam's mother hands her a jar of fig jam. Together they walk out into the starry night. They pass the synagogue and come to a part of the city Miriam has never seen before.

"What is that?" She points to a building with a dome and high tower.

"It's the mosque, where our Muslim neighbors pray."

Miriam and her mother stop at a gate covered with vines of night-blooming jasmine. A woman comes into the courtyard, followed by a girl Miriam's age.

"Salaam!"

"Salaam!"

The mothers kiss each other's cheeks.

"I brought you some jam," Miriam's mother says.

"Thank you. Would your daughter like to help my daughter Jasmine pick flowers for the tea?"

The woman's voice is kind, but her accent sounds strange to Miriam. She shakes her head and clings to her mother's hand.

Jasmine plucks a handful of sweet-smelling blossoms and tosses them into the teapot. Miriam inhales the flowery steam. The girls peep at each other while their mothers chat. When the teapot is empty, Jasmine's mother tells her to get two sacks of flour from the storeroom.

"Why two?"

"One for us and one for our guests."

"Miriam, help Jasmine carry the flour."

Jasmine skips ahead. Miriam follows her. Jasmine disappears inside a storeroom and brings out two sacks of flour.

"Why don't you have any flour at your house?" Jasmine asks.

Miriam shrugs, embarrassed. She takes a sack of flour and hurries back. Miriam can run across her own courtyard easily, even at night, but here in the unfamiliar courtyard, she catches her toe on a stone and almost falls.

Jasmine catches the sack of flour just in time.

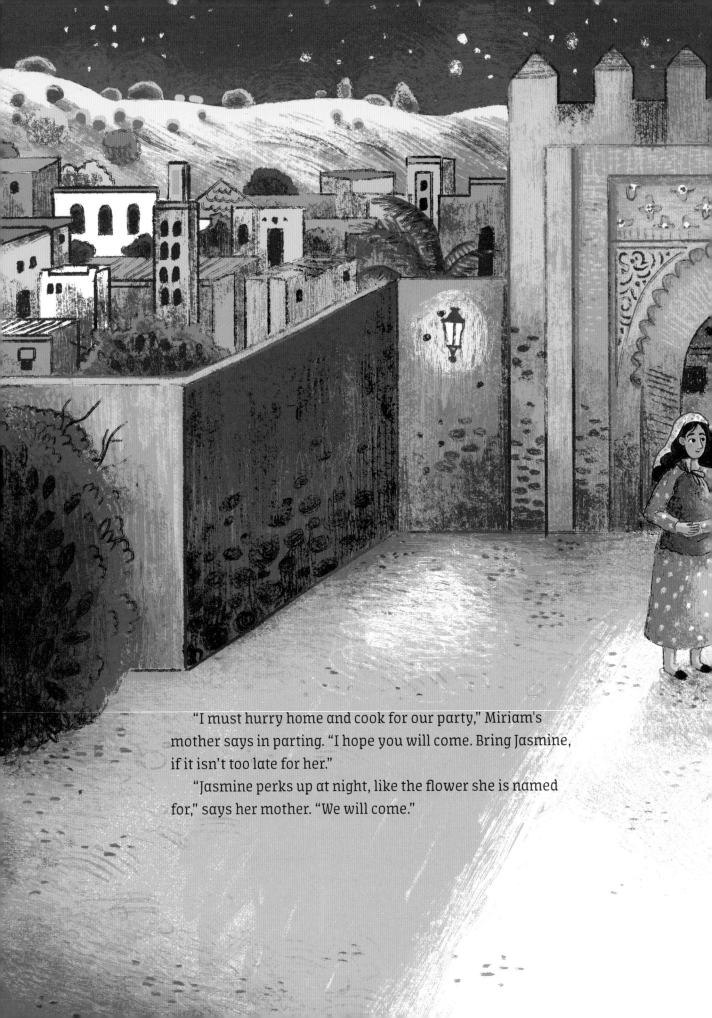

"I must hurry home and cook for our party," Miriam's mother says in parting. "I hope you will come. Bring Jasmine, if it isn't too late for her."

"Jasmine perks up at night, like the flower she is named for," says her mother. "We will come."

When they get back to their own street, Miriam lets forth a stream of questions. "How did you know to go to that house? How did she know we were coming? How did she know we wanted flour?"

"I go there every year to get flour for Mimouna."

They reach their home.

"Why don't we have a jasmine vine?"

"I will get a clipping for you to plant."

Miriam's mother begins mixing the batter. Miriam decorates the table. She arranges stalks of green wheat in a vase. She sets out a jug brimming with olive oil, and plates of fish and dried fruits and nuts. Her father hands her five gold coins to arrange around the edge of a bowl filled with flour. He gives the traditional Mimouna blessing, "A year of plenty and good luck!"

"We have plenty." Miriam looks at the table. "Do we also have luck?"

"See if you have luck getting your little brother into his party clothes," her mother says.

Miriam puts on her holiday dress. She succeeds in wriggling her brother's arms into his sleeves just as the guests begin to arrive.

By the time Jasmine and her parents come to the door, the house is full of family and friends. Miriam is in the courtyard, where people are playing drums and singing "Alalla Mimouna." Jasmine stays by the door, clinging to her mother's hand. Miriam knows she should welcome her guest, but she feels shy.

Soon the scent of frying dough draws Miriam to the kitchen.
Her mother flips the first golden-brown moufletot onto a plate
and spreads them with butter and jam.

Miriam's mouth waters. "Who are those for?"

"You can take these to your grandfather."

Plate in hand, she walks toward her grandfather, who sits at the head of the holiday table. Suddenly, her slipper catches on the edge of the carpet. She stumbles. The dripping stack of moufletot fly toward her grandfather's gold-embroidered robe!

Jasmine catches the plate just in time.

Miriam didn't even notice she was standing nearby.

Her grandfather wipes up the drop of fig jam that fell on his robe and licks it off his finger.

"Did you girls plan that lovely dance routine?" he asks with a smile.

The girls laugh as they hand him the plate. Miriam gets her tambourine and teaches Jasmine the song "Alalla Mimouna."

Miriam's mother fills another plate with pancakes. "You may give this one to Jasmine. You were certainly lucky she was close by."

When the serving platters are empty, everyone goes next door. On Mimouna, the whole neighborhood celebrates together. The party moves from house to house. Everyone is singing, dancing, laughing and eating. A neighbor serves fresh couscous. One aunt made sesame cookies.

Jasmine tastes a piece of leftover matzah. "It's good," she says, crunching. Miriam has another cookie instead.

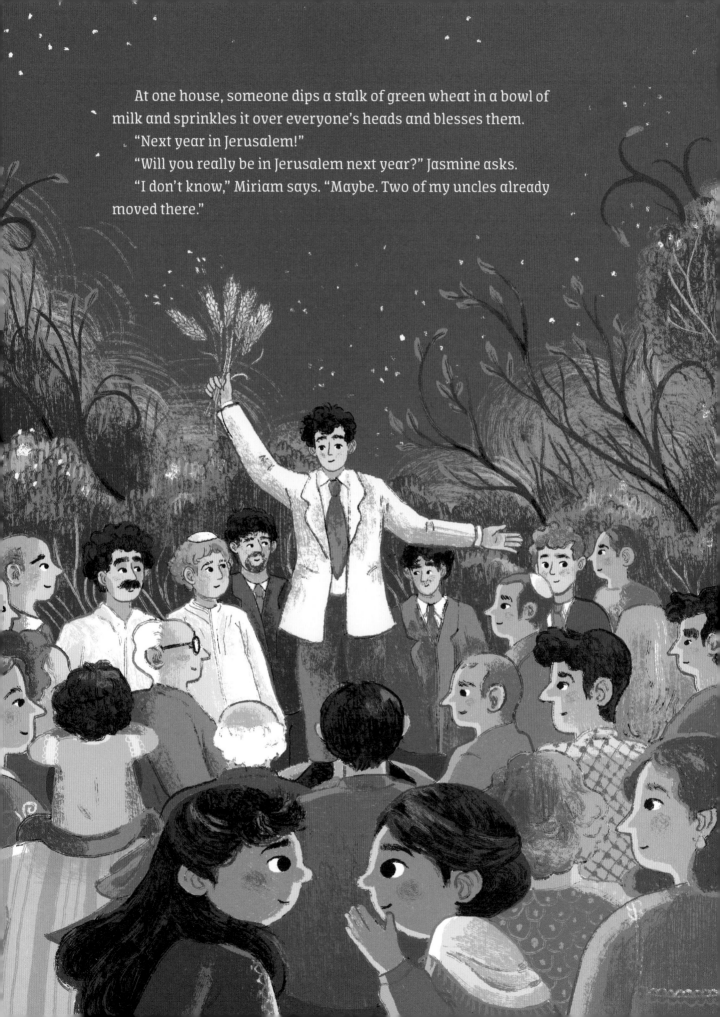

At one house, someone dips a stalk of green wheat in a bowl of milk and sprinkles it over everyone's heads and blesses them.

"Next year in Jerusalem!"

"Will you really be in Jerusalem next year?" Jasmine asks.

"I don't know," Miriam says. "Maybe. Two of my uncles already moved there."

It is after midnight when they get back to Miriam's house. The girls share one last pancake.

"This reminds me of our Ramadan holiday," Jasmine says. "We fast every day and have big meals at night. Maybe you will come to our Ramadan party?"

"Maybe I will." Miriam turns to her mother. "Can we go to Jasmine's Ramadan party sometime?"

"I am not sure."

"Why not?"

"We might not live in Morocco by then. We may be in Jerusalem."

The tired girls lie down on a pile of pillows, giggle
together a little bit, then quickly fall asleep.

One year later, on the last day of Passover, Miriam sits on her balcony and watches the sky above the rooftops of Jerusalem turn dark.

When three stars twinkle overhead, she runs into their new apartment.

"I want to help make the moufletot! But where can we get flour now?"

Her mother hands her a few coins. "The store on the corner
will open soon."

Miriam skips easily down the now-familiar city street singing
"Alalla Mimouna . . ."

When she gets back, the apartment is filled with family and friends. The sweet smell of moufletot mingles with the scent of the night-blooming jasmine vine on the porch.

Miriam remembers the Mimouna party in her old neighborhood in Morocco and wonders if Jasmine is waiting for her to come get a sack of flour.

What Is Mimouna?

Mimouna is a Jewish holiday that takes place the day after the week-long Passover festival ends. These holidays occur in the spring, during the Hebrew month of Nissan. Mimouna is a relatively recent addition to the cycle of Jewish holidays, and little is known about its origins. It was first celebrated about two hundred and fifty years ago by Jewish communities in Morocco and other parts of North Africa.

According to Jewish tradition, during Passover it is forbidden to eat foods made from flour, except for quickly baked, unleavened matzah crackers. On Mimouna, bread and other doughy treats can be eaten again. This is a great excuse for a festive meal — but getting flour in the evening, as soon as Passover ends, hasn't always been simple. In the past, some Jewish families in Morocco would ask their Muslim neighbors for flour and invite them to their Mimouna party. During Mimouna celebrations, blessings are given for a year of prosperity and good luck.

Today, there is only a small Jewish population in Morocco, but Mimouna celebrations are becoming more popular in Israel and around the world, primarily among Jewish communities of Sephardic/Mizrahi (Eastern) background. The paper-thin pancakes called moufletot are a favorite Mimouna treat. To host your own Mimouna party, follow the simple recipe on the next page . . . then reach beyond your usual group of friends and invite someone new to enjoy them with you!

Moufletot

Unlike matzah (the unleavened bread eaten during Passover), moufletot are made with yeast and are allowed to rise.

1 ½ cups warm water	1 teaspoon salt
2 teaspoons dry yeast	1 large egg, beaten
4 cups flour	Cooking oil
1/3 cup sugar	

Ask an adult to help you make the moufletot.

Pour the warm (not hot) water in a large bowl. Sprinkle the yeast on the warm water and wait a few minutes until it gets bubbly.

Mix in the flour, sugar, salt and egg until well combined, then knead for a few minutes. If the dough is too sticky to handle easily, add a little more flour.

Divide the dough into golf ball–sized portions. Place them on a plate or tray, leaving a little space between them so they can expand. Drizzle a little cooking oil over the balls and turn them so they are lightly coated with oil. Let them rise for 20 minutes.

Pat or roll one ball into a very thin circle. Make it as thin as possible without tearing.

Heat a teaspoon of oil in a cast iron or non-stick frying pan on medium heat.

Fry the first moufleta for 2 minutes, then flip and fry for another 2 minutes. (Note: this is the only one that is fried on both sides.) While the first one is frying, roll out the second moufleta. Place the second moufleta on top of the first. Carefully flip them together.

Continue rolling out and adding moufletot to the stack. Each time, add a few drops of oil as needed, fry for 2 minutes, then carefully flip the whole stack together. When the stack gets too large to flip easily, start another stack.

Serve warm. Peel a moufleta off the top of the stack. Spread it with butter and honey or jam. Roll it up, tucking in the ends, and enjoy!

MAKES ABOUT 30 MOUFLETOT.

Recipe courtesy of the Samama family in Shefer, Israel.

**To the memory of Dr. Erik H. Cohen,
who taught me much and introduced me to the traditions of Mimouna.**

Thanks to all the people who generously gave their time in sharing their knowledge and memories of Mimouna in Morocco, especially Judith Cohen, Suzanne Benchimol and Vanessa Paloma of KHOYA: Jewish Morocco Sound Archive, Casablanca, Morocco. Special thanks to Devorah Busheri for her translation of the English text into Hebrew for the version published by Kinneret, Zmora, Dvir — Publishing House Ltd.

Published in English in Canada and the USA in 2020 by Groundwood Books
First published in Hebrew in 2019 as *A Sack of Luck: A Mimouna Night Tale* by
Kinneret, Zmora, Dvir — Publishing House Ltd.
English translation rights arranged through
S.B. Rights Agency — Stephanie Barrouillet

Groundwood Books would like to thank Rabbi Daniel J. Feder
for checking the manuscript.

Groundwood Books / House of Anansi Press
groundwoodbooks.com

We gratefully acknowledge the Government of Canada
for its financial support of our publishing program.

With the participation of the Government of Canada
Avec la participation du gouvernement du Canada | Canadä

Library and Archives Canada Cataloguing in Publication
Title: A sweet meeting on Mimouna night / Allison Ofanansky ;
illustrated by Rotem Teplow.
Names: Ofanansky, Allison, author. | Teplow, Rotem, illustrator.
Identifiers: Canadiana (print) 20200167081 | Canadiana (ebook) 2020016709X |
ISBN 9781773063973 (hardcover) | ISBN 9781773063980 (EPUB) |
ISBN 9781773063997 (Kindle)
Classification: LCC PZ7.O37 Sw 2020 | DDC j813/.6—dc239

The illustrations were created in Photoshop.
Design by Sara Loos and Michael Solomon
Printed and bound in China

FSC
www.fsc.org
MIX
Paper from
responsible sources
FSC® C144853